THE IRISH PIPER

THE IRISH PIPER

JIM LATIMER
Pictures by JOHN O'BRIEN

CHARLES SCRIBNER'S SONS · NEW YORK
Collier Macmillan Canada · Toronto
Maxwell Macmillan International Publishing Group
New York · Oxford · Singapore · Sydney

For Martin Hayes and Willie Clancy

—J. L.

To Tess

—J. O'B.

Once upon a time there was a piper, a man who played the Irish pipes, though he also played the Irish flute and whistles. The piper's flute and his pipes were made of wood. His whistles were made of tin. The piper dressed in colorful patchwork, so he was sometimes called the Pied Piper. The Pied Piper lived in County Clare, in the west of Ireland.

Now this Irish piper played lovely music on the flute, the whistles, and the pipes. He played splendid, lively music, music more lively and more vivid than any you can probably imagine. For example, when the piper was feeling sad, when he played sad pipe music, his music was so sad it could make a group of gruff, grown men suddenly burst into tears.

And when the piper was feeling strong, when he played strong march music, he could make frail ladies—and I mean fragile, thin ladies—beat up their mean husbands. His strong music could cause little husbands to stand up and talk back to their wives, even when the wives were black-smiths and hammer throwers.

And when the piper felt like flying, when he played his bird music, you could actually feel feathers forming on your arms and down the back of your neck. After a while you would even feel you had a beak—and a tail. That's how good—that's how *vivid*—the piper's bird music was. And we're talking about the Irish Pied Piper from County Clare in the west of Ireland.

But—this is a big "but"—while the piper's bird music and his sad and strong music were good, while they were all very good, none of this music was his best. It was not the type of music that made you want to change your name and pack up your clothes and leave your lovely mother or father. It was not the type of music that made you want to run away and never come back home again. No, only the music that was the Pied Piper's particular specialty could do these things.

His specialty music, one kind, was about cheese, about Irish cheese and bacon. The piper's other special music was about balloons, about strange balloons and butterflies and carousels. His cheese-and-bacon music was a reel, his balloon-and-butterfly music was a jig, and when the Irish piper played this music, his special reel or his special jig—well, you'll see what happened. Because it did happen once in Hamelin, in Germany, when the town of Hamelin had a lot of rats.

In fact, this is going to be mainly a rat story, a story about the Pied Piper from County Clare and about the time he went over to Hamelin, in Saxony, in the north of Germany, when Hamelin was overwhelmed with rats. And these were loose-limbed, long-tailed, brown- and gray- and black-furred rats. The rats of Hamelin, Germany.

In lower Saxony, in the north and west of Germany, on the lovely Weser River in a valley surrounded by rolling, wooded hills, lies the lovely town of Hamelin. But at the time this story begins, Hamelin was not a lovely place to live. It was a place of self-centered citizens, with a mean but clever mayor, with a foolish magistrate, and with lackluster, dull-witted aldermen, though the head alderman's daughter was very nice. Come to think of it, most of the citizens of Hamelin had *children* who were nice. But the most distressing thing about Hamelin, the most unlovely thing, was its rats.

There were rats in the Hamelin churchyards and clock towers. There were rats asleep in shower stalls and rats browsing on bookshelves. On a typical day you would probably find a gray rat hiding under your hat brim, or a brown or black rat (maybe one of each) crawling up your coat sleeve. In your pantry you would probably find jam footprints—*rat* jam footprints—on your shelves, and you might find rat *flour* footprints in your jam. There would probably be rats crawling through the coleslaw and rats making a mess of the margarine. And there would be rats snarling your shoelaces, rats making a wreck of your ribbons, and rats leaping about in your laundry. And the citizens of Hamelin—you can hardly blame them—were growing restless.

The mayor, meeting with her council, with her aldermen and her magistrate, was addressing the Rat Question.

The head alderman was speaking to the mayor. "Your most gracious honor," he said, "we must do something. We must pass a resolution. We must pass an *appropriation.*"

The mayor smiled. "We must have something stronger than an appropriation," she said.

"What?" the aldermen shouted together.

"Poison," answered the mayor. "Or else," she said, still smiling, "we must have a piper. We must have the *Pied* Piper."

The aldermen stared.

The magistrate stared.

"No," said the head alderman. "With due respect, gracious honor, we could never find enough poison or poison strong enough. And as for the piper," he said, "the Pied Piper is only a story. There is no real Pied Piper."

It was at this moment—at just this moment—that there came a knock on the chamber door.

There was silence in the council.

The knock came again. It was a *musical* knock. Possibly a piper's knock. Indeed, it was the Pied Piper, our patchwork Pied Piper from County Clare in Ireland. The council chamberlain opened the door and ushered him in.

"Who are you?" the mayor asked him, though she could see perfectly well who he was.

"I'm the Pied Piper," he said.

The aldermen stared. The magistrate stared.

"I've come for your rats," he said.

"You've come to lead all of the rats of Hamelin right out of town," the mayor corrected him.

The piper nodded.

The mayor smiled. "And you're going to do this with your pipes."

"Yes, by playing these pipes," said the piper.

The mayor smiled at her aldermen and her magistrate. "Wonderful," she said. "Of course, we will have to have a demonstration."

Without a word the piper started to play. He played his sad music, and there was quiet in the mayor's council. Even the rats, pawing and scratching beneath the baseboards, grew quiet. The aldermen listened to the piper's sad music, blinking back tears. The magistrate wept openly, crying, "Oh, my—oh, mercy and gracious!"

Then the piper changed to his strong music. Instantly the mayor and council were galvanized. In their minds' eyes, as they listened, the councilmen were heroes and great champions, marching in a parade. The magistrate actually came up out of his chair and marched around the council chamber in rhythm. And yet, as they listened, the mayor and her aldermen grew strangely uncomfortable, for they were all mean husbands (the mayor was a mean wife), and the piper's strong music seemed to tell them their *wives* (and the mayor's husband) were becoming galvanized. As they listened, a slight anxiety began to stir inside them.

And then the piper played his bird music. The aldermen felt the backs of their necks and the backs of their arms. Their anxiety grew stronger. Feathers seemed to be forming—seemed to be sprouting on the aldermen. But *could* they be? The magistrate leaped from his chair and began to hop and flap about. "I'm actually *flying,*" he cried, hopping and flapping around the room.

The aldermen were now altogether frightened. Even the mayor was alarmed. "ENOUGH," she shouted at the piper. "That is *enough,*" she said.

The piper stopped playing. The mayor took a breath. She recovered her composure. "We accept your proposition," she said, and smiled. "Actually," she told the piper, "if you will do this, if you will clear the rats out of Hamelin and drown them in the river, we will give you a cornucopia of treasures and rewards."

The piper blinked at her.

"We will make you…" The mayor paused. "We will make you an honorary citizen—an honorary *alderman* for life."

The aldermen gasped.

"We will…" The mayor paused. "We will make your birthday a holiday. We will have our best writer write a story about you—maybe a poem.

"And we will give you a lot of jewelry," the mayor continued. "Earrings. Or plain rings. And bracelets.

"Finally," she concluded, "we will arrange an appointment for you with the head alderman's lovely daughter." The mayor winked at the piper. "She is a musician like yourself—a wonderful performer on the violin. Her name is Gretchen."

The head alderman stifled a cry. His daughter, Gretchen, wrote his speeches and his letters for him and fixed him his breakfast. He had never allowed her to have an appointment with a young man.

The piper, meanwhile, had listened to the mayor's long recital in silence. He did not much care for earrings or plain rings or bracelets. He had come to beguile the rats of Hamelin mostly for fun. And yet he had already made up his mind to meet this Gretchen. Her fiddle playing, which he had noticed on his way into town, was maybe the best he had ever heard. So the piper accepted the mayor's offer.

"Done," he said.

The mayor smiled and shook the piper's hand, and then turned a stern, warning look on the magistrate and the aldermen, who sat in stunned silence. Making the piper an honorary alderman was almost unimaginably shocking, but making his birthday a holiday, giving him jewelry and an appointment with Gretchen—the magistrate and aldermen were speechless at the thought of these things.

Moments later the Pied Piper appeared at the edge of the Hamelin square. The magistrate, aldermen, and mayor hurried to the council-chamber window to watch. The piper began to play, and the rats, instantly aware of him, began to come out. From behind bushes and under doorsteps, they came—from clock towers and storm drains, from bedchambers and broom corners. The mayor's council watched, astonished, as rangy, long-limbed rats by the scores and hundreds walked into the town square. And while they were ill-fit and unkempt, the rats were *dressed.* Some in checks or stripes. Some in houndstooth or paisley. One group was particularly unkempt and slatternly looking. They were chewing gum, walking on hind legs with paws in their pockets. When all of the rats had assembled, this group stepped forward.

The piper stopped playing. The head rat spat out his gum, took a fresh stick from his pocket, and folded it with his paw. "We have heard of you," he said in a rasping voice. "We have heard this story before. And we are not going to follow you." The head rat put the fresh gum into his mouth. "No way," he said, and resumed chewing. The head rat's companions scratched themselves and gazed about, looking nonchalant and bored. The piper played his sad music. He played his strong music and his bird music. If the rats felt saddened or galvanized or feathered, they showed no sign of it. Instead they chewed their gum and seemed to snicker among themselves.

"Very nice," said the head rat. "We must look for you to play the next time there's a rat wedding."

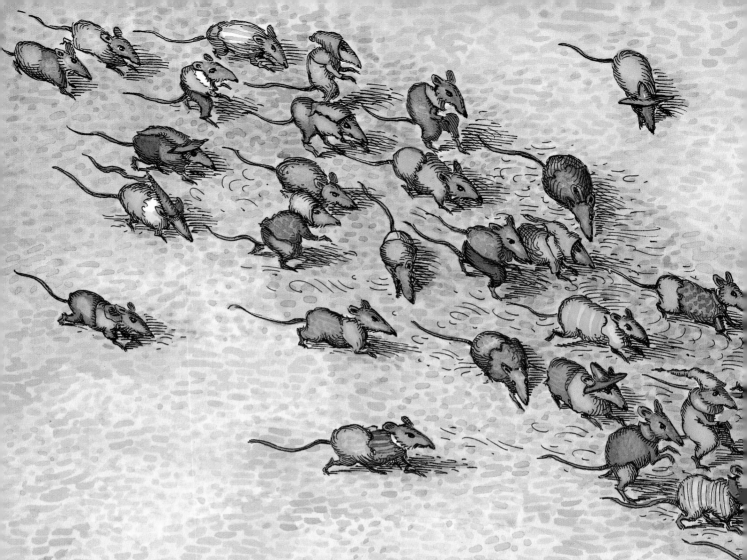

But the piper did not answer. He continued to play, and gradually, very subtly and gradually, a change came into his music. And subtly and gradually, a change came over the rats, too.

The change was evident first among the rats who were chewing gum. They stopped chewing. They stopped gazing about and looking nonchalant. Gradually all of the rats in the square grew alert. They were staring at the piper now—and listening. The head rat was trying to put into words exactly what this music sounded like to him. It sounded like kitchens. No, like something *in* a kitchen. The piper's music sounded like *cheese*. Indeed it *tasted* like cheese. Like lovely Irish cheese and—and Irish bacon.

The Pied Piper's music, with its kitcheny sound and beckoning taste, percolated through the gathering. It was alluring. It was intoxicating. Soon the rats felt almost drunk with bacon and cheese.

"Let's follow him!" shouted the head rat, for the piper had turned away from the square and started to make his way out of town.

"Hooray!" came a cheer from the rat-gathering, and amid shouts of "Let's follow him" and "We're out of here," the rats followed the piper out of the square and out of town, toward the river and the wooded hills beyond.

The mayor and council, meanwhile, had been watching from their window overlooking the square. They watched as the rat procession gradually disappeared toward the hills beyond the river. When the last rat had departed, the mayor turned to her aldermen with an expression that was sly and satisfied. The magistrate moved among his colleagues, winking and grinning and elbowing them in the ribs. "Gone," he said. "They're gone forever." But very soon a feeling of doubt began to creep into the minds of the aldermen. At first just a slight anxiety, the doubt grew into alarm, then dismay.

"What?" the mayor barked at them, sensing their alarm and preparing to be cross. "Now what?" she said.

"Now we must *pay* him," said the second head alderman, who was a jeweler. "Now we must give this piper a cornucopia of—of *earrings*. And *bracelets*."

The head alderman sighed. The mayor had promised the piper an appointment with his daughter, the precious daughter who wrote his letters and speeches for him and made him his breakfast. He sighed again.

"And we must make him an *alderman,*" the third head alderman was saying.

"We must make his birthday a *holiday,*" said the fourth.

"And if we do not do these things," said the fifth, "he will entice our children away, just as he did the rats."

"Stop!" shouted the mayor. "That is just a story. The piper will *not* entice our children away. There is no way he will ever do that."

The magistrate and aldermen sat down and waited for the mayor to explain. She looked at them narrowly. "How many children do we have in Hamelin, would you say?" she asked.

"Oh," replied the magistrate, "somewhere around five hundred. They're mostly brats," he added.

"Yes, mostly brats," the mayor replied. "And can you imagine what it would be like traveling about the countryside with around five hundred brats? It would be a nightmare, a *piper's* nightmare."

The aldermen and the magistrate thought about it.

"It is not going to happen," the mayor concluded. "No, gentlemen, your jewelry and your holidays, your children—your daughter, my good sir" (this she addressed to the head alderman)—"all are quite safe." The mayor smiled at them. "Depend upon it," she said. "Children follow pipers in stories, but not in life."

The mayor was wrong, though. Children *do* follow pipers if the pipers are very good and if the children live in a town whose mayor and aldermen are as awful as these aldermen and this mayor were. And the head alderman's daughter was not safe. She liked the piper almost at once. She liked his Irish tunes. And she loved the Hamelin children, though some *were* brats. The holidays of Hamelin, its jewelry, and the honorary place on its council—all of these things *would* have been safe, for the piper did not care about them. But the aldermen and the magistrate and mayor provoked him. Here is how it happened.

When the piper came back from the hills beyond the river, the mayor and aldermen declared they were not going to reward him for leading the rats away. They would not give him his jewelry, his holiday, his appointment with the head alderman's daughter. "And if you think you are going to entice our children away," the mayor told him, "go ahead. They are mostly brats," she said. "They are a piper's nightmare. So just go ahead."

"Okay," said the piper.

Moments later the Pied Piper and Gretchen, the head alderman's daughter, appeared together in the Hamelin square. Gretchen had brought her fiddle. Together Gretchen and the piper began to play a jig, one they had practiced while the piper was on his way back from leading the rats out of town. It may have been the slipjig we now call "The Butterfly." Soon the air seemed to crackle and spark with music, and soon the square was filled with the sound of dancing feet in wooden shoes, the shoes of ruddy-cheeked, curly haired children.

To the children, the music sounded like butterflies and carousels, like ribbons and strange balloons. With the piper and Gretchen leading, they danced out of the square, and out of town, and into the wooded hills. And as the mayor and her astonished aldermen watched, the hills seemed to part and let the piper and the children and Gretchen through—and then to close back up again behind them.

The Hamelin children disappeared (all but the few who *were* brats, who stayed behind), and they did not come back. Where they went and what became of them is a mystery in Hamelin right up to the present day. Some of the citizens of Hamelin believe the children went to England, where, years later, their memory came into the mind and into the poetry of Mr. Robert Browning. But in the west of Ireland, in County Clare, some children—some ruddy-cheeked, curly haired, Saxon-looking children— still dance in wooden shoes to "The Butterfly." They dance to music played on the fiddle and the pipes—and sometimes on the Irish flute and whistles.

AUTHOR'S NOTE

The Oxford Companion to Children's Literature tells an old Pied Piper story, a story written by a German monk 540 years ago. The monk's name was Heinrich von Herford. He was a Dominican and an historian. Von Herford's story, written about 1450, is our earliest record of the Pied Piper of Hameln, Germany. (It was the English poet Robert Browning, writing nearly 400 years later, who added the syllable that changed Hameln to Hamelin.)

In the year 1284, according to Heinrich von Herford, on June 16, a mysterious, handsome piper, a flute player, appeared at the Hameln gate. The piper had crossed the bridge over the Weser River. He passed through the Weser Gate and began to play. The piper played such strong, alluring music that all of the children within hearing immediately began to follow him. The piper led the Hameln children back out through the Weser Gate and over the bridge, and then he disappeared. The Hameln children, about 130 of them, disappeared, too. No one knew where the handsome piper had come from. No news of him or of the Hameln children was ever heard again.

Can Heinrich von Herford's story be true? Was there really a Pied Piper? Can there be music so vivid and so alluring it might have caused 130 children to follow a piper and never return home again? We don't know. We don't know what really

happened in Hameln in June of 1284, and we don't know very much about the popular music of the thirteenth century. We don't know how or why the piper came to be a rat catcher, though we think we know when. The rats seem to have come into the story during the sixteenth century, in the south of Germany.

Do we know anything else about the Pied Piper of Hameln or about his music? Not very much. And yet we have—this author has—a speculation about the music. The traditional music of Ireland is strong and alluring. Traditional Irish music of the present day was popular music of old, and we think the origins of this music may go back to the thirteenth century.

There is a strong style of music found near Ennis in Ireland, in the region north of Limerick, near the Slieve Aughty Mountains, in the Lakelands of County Clare. The music of Clare, especially as played in the villages of Tulla and Feakle, is magical and alluring. Clare music has grace and freedom. It has breathless energy and heart-stopping rhythm. It is music that might have charmed rats and children. The music of County Clare, in the west of Ireland, heard suddenly in Saxony in June of the year 1284, might easily have charmed all of the rats and all of the children of Hameln.

Thanks to Sherry Wohlers Ladig, Daithi Sproule, Paddy O'Brien, Laura Mackenzie, Ann Heymann, Leo Rickertsen, and Ron Runeborg.

Library of Congress Cataloging-in-Publication Data.
Latimer, Jim, 1943–   The Irish piper / Jim Latimer; pictures by John O'Brien.—1st ed. p. cm.   Summary: In this version of the traditional tale, the Pied Piper plays upon Irish pipes and travels from County Clare in Ireland to the village of Hamelin to rid it of its rats. An author's note discusses the piper's music. 1. Pied Piper of Hamelin (Legendary character) [1. Pied Piper of Hamelin (Legendary character) 2. Folklore—Germany (West)—Hameln.] I. O'Brien, John, 1953–   ill. II. Title. PZ8.1.L335Ir 1991   398.2—dc20   [E] 90–34550   CIP   AC   ISBN 0–684–19130–X